I'm Not Afraid of This Haunted House

by Laurie Friedman

illustrations by Teresa Murfin

Carolrhoda Books, Inc. / Minneapolis

For Dana,
the bravest
of the brave
—L.B.F.

For my family,
my friends,
and for Alison
—T.M.

Text copyright © 2005 by Laurie B. Friedman
Illustrations copyright © 2005 by Teresa Murfin

Carolrhoda Books, Inc.
A division of Lerner Publishing Group
241 First Avenue North
Minneapolis, MN 55401 U.S.A.

Website address: www.lernerbooks.com

Library of Congress Cataloging-in-Publication Data

Friedman, Laurie B.
    I'm not afraid of this haunted house / by Laurie Friedman : illustrations by Teresa Murfin.
        p.   cm.
    Summary: Simon Lester Henry Strauss is not in the least afraid of any haunted house, but there is something else that terrifies him.
    ISBN-13: 978-1-57505-751-4 (lib. bdg. : alk. paper)
    ISBN-10: 1-57505-751-4 (lib. bdg. : alk. paper)
    [1. Haunted houses—Fiction. 2. Fear—Fiction. 3. Stories in rhyme.] I. Title: I am not afraid of this haunted house. II. Murfin, Teresa, ill. III. Title.
PZ8.3.F91164Im 2005
[E]—dc22
                                                        2004031078

Manufactured in the United States of America
1 2 3 4 5 6 — JR — 10 09 08 07 06 05

"I'm Simon Lester Henry Strauss,
and I'm not afraid of this haunted house."

A fortune teller says, "Come inside."
Her crystal ball says, "You can't hide."

My friends are scared of what they'll see.
But I just tell them, "Follow me!
I'm Simon Lester Henry Strauss,
and I'm not afraid of this haunted house."

I'm not afraid of the witch at the door.
I'm not afraid of the creaky old floor.

When a ghost swoops down
and hollers, "**BOO!**"
I shout back,
"I'm not scared of you!"

I'm not afraid at the Vampire's Feast.
I can handle these bloodsucking beasts!

I bare my neck and face my fate.
I help myself to a dinner plate.
"I'm Simon Lester Henry Strauss,
and I'm not afraid of this haunted house."

I'm not afraid of the screaming ghoul.
I tell him that his tunes sound cool.

The bloody werewolf
makes me laugh.
I point him to the
nearest bath.

I'm not afraid of the goblin in bed,
who's snacking on spiders that hang overhead.

My friends start running left and right.
But I reach up and take a bite.
"I'm Simon Lester Henry Strauss,
and I'm not afraid of this haunted house."

In the graveyard,
by the light of the moon,
a skeleton hums an ominous tune.

My friends start screaming when he moans,
but I shake hands with that old bag of bones.
"I'm Simon Lester Henry Strauss,
and I'm not afraid of this haunted house."

I'm not afraid when a wedding takes place,
and Frankenstein's bride can't find her face.

My friends all hide, but I just smile
and cheer the couple down the aisle.

At the reception, I try
blood and brains.
For dessert, I sample
guts and veins.

When a one-eyed monster pops out of the cake
and says, "Who wants to rattle and shake?"
my friends look like they'll wet their pants,
but I grab her arm and start to dance.

"I'm Simon Lester
Henry Strauss,
and I'm not afraid of this
haunted house."

In the distance, I see something cool—
the Treacherous Tower and the Vampire's Pool.
My friends all scream, "Come on! Let's run!"
But I march inside. This looks like fun!

There's nothing here that scares me at all.
Not the rows of coffins that line the wall.

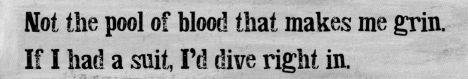

Not the pool of blood that makes me grin.
If I had a suit, I'd dive right in.

I'm not afraid when the room goes black.
Not a sliver of light peeks through a crack.

But I'm not scared. Oh no, not me!
PITCH BLACK is my favorite place to be.

I'm not even scared of the moving floor.
My friends cry, "We can't take any more!"

I laugh as they tremble and pitch a fit.
There's nothing here that scares me one bit!

Outside, my friends collapse in fear.
But I can't wait to come back next year!

I raise my hands up to the sky and cry out loud,
"I'M ONE BRAVE GUY!
I'M SIMON LESTER HENRY STRAUSS,
AND I'M NOT AFRAID OF THIS . . .

"EEEEEEEEEEEEEEK...

A
MOUSE!"

Way Out